Damon Burnard

A division of Hodder Headline Limited

To Sara and Channa, and Jimmy the Fat, Lazy Cat

First published as a My First Read Alone
in Great Britain in 2000
by Hodder Children's Books

10 9 8 7 6 5 4

 A Catalogue record for this book is available from the British Library

ISBN 0 340 78778 3

Printed and bound by Omnia Books Ltd, Glasgow

Hodder Children's Books
a division of Hodder Headline Limited
338 Euston Road
London NW1 3BH

Visit Damon's website!
http://home1.gte.net/dburnard

Cindy the centipede lived in a kitchen. Can you find her?

Here's a clue: she's under the table!

Here's Cindy close-up . . .

As you can see, she had LOTS of arms and legs.

Cindy had SO many arms and legs, that they often got in her way. Sometimes she knocked things over . . .

. . . dropped things . . .

. . . and tripped up.

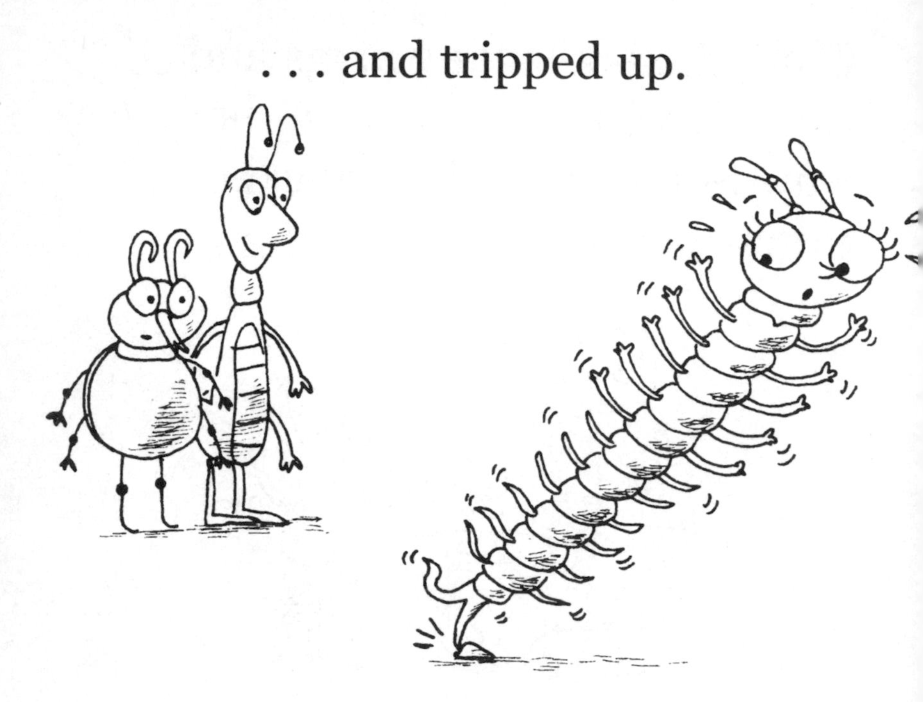

She just couldn't help it!

Sometimes the other bugs called her names.
'Clumsy!' they said.
'Butterfingers!' they laughed.

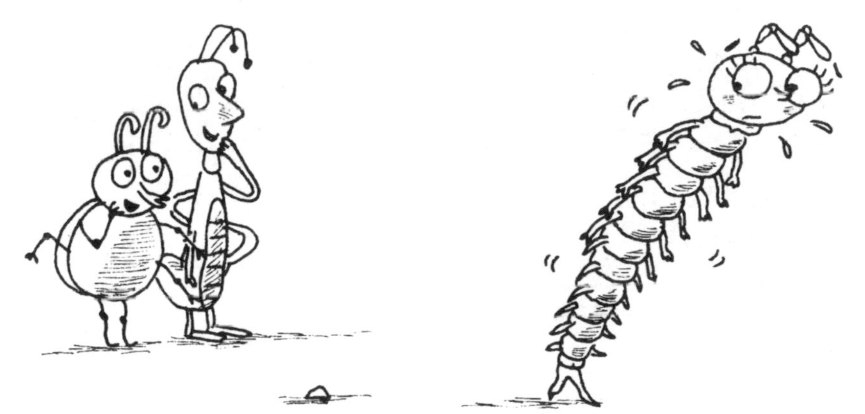

They were only joking, but they hurt Cindy's feelings all the same.
'I wish I had just eight arms and legs like other bugs,' she sighed.
'I wish I wasn't a centipede!'

One day Cindy called on her friend, Frank Fly.

'Hi, Frank!' said Cindy. 'What are you doing today?'

‘I’m going swimming,’ said Frank. ‘Would you like to come?’
‘I’m not sure,’ said Cindy. ‘I’ve never been swimming before!’

‘Oh, it’s easy-peasy!’ said Frank.
‘Really?’ said Cindy. ‘Well, in that case . . .’

Off they went, across the kitchen.
Then they came to the sink.

It was FULL of bugs swimming!

'Hi, Frank! Hi, Cindy!' they shouted.
'Come on in, the water's lovely!'

'YIPPEEE!'

yelled Frank.
And he jumped straight in!

Cindy dipped a toe in the water. It felt nice and warm, but she was scared.

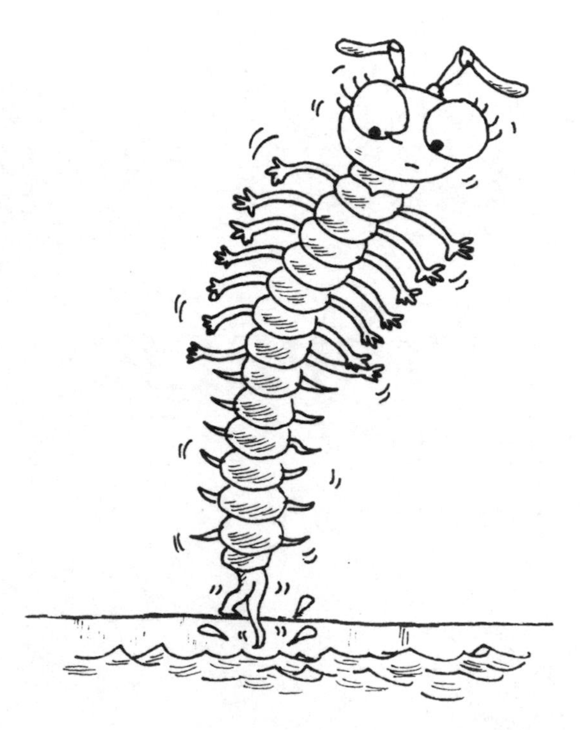

'Come on Cindy!' shouted Frank.

‘I’m not sure . . .’ said Cindy.
She took a step backwards.
But as she did . . .

. . . she tripped.

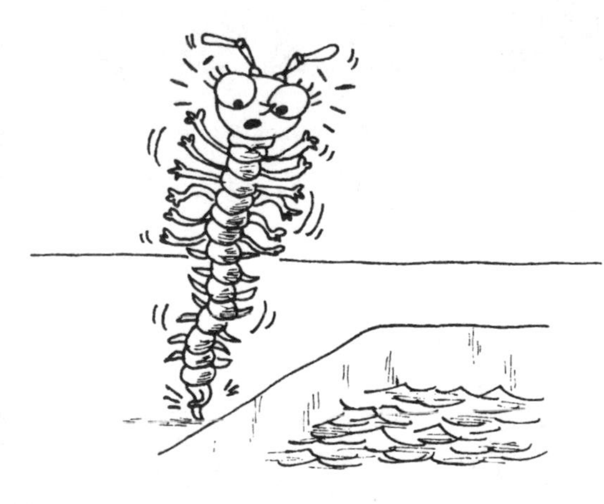

And then . . .

Into the sink she fell!

cried Cindy, splashing her arms and legs.

‘STOP!’ yelled the other bugs.
‘You’re making waves!’

But Cindy splashed even more.

‘Don’t panic!’ said Frank.
He helped Cindy to the side.

'Thanks, Frank!' puffed Cindy.
'You're welcome!' smiled Frank.
But some of the other bugs
weren't smiling.
'Hey, Clumsy!' shouted Anita Ant.
'Come back when you know how
to swim!'

'Don't worry, Cindy,' said Frank.
'Try again. I'll help you!'
'Maybe later,' said Cindy.

Cindy sat behind a cup.
She heard the others swimming about, having fun.

'I hate being a centipede,' she sighed.

She looked around the kitchen. Jimmy, the fat, lazy cat, was asleep on the floor, next to his saucer of milk.

Cindy had a great idea.

'I'll show Anita!' she thought. 'I'll teach myself to be the best swimmer ever!'

She skipped to the saucer . . .

. . . and stood on the edge . . .

. . . and she jumped - straight into the middle!

‘Ha!’ thought Cindy. ‘That was easy-peasy!’

But the milk was deeper than it looked . . .

‘HELP!’ she cried. ‘I CAN’T TOUCH THE BOTTOM!’
But no one heard her.

She splished . . .

. . . she splashed . . .

. . . she kicked . . .

. . . and thrashed . . .

But hard as she tried, Cindy could not swim back to the side . . .

And all the while her arms and legs were getting very, VERY tired!

Back at the sink, Frank was getting worried. Cindy had been gone for a long time.

'I must find her,' he thought, 'and make sure she's OK.'

He dried himself off . . .

. . . and buzzed over to Cindy's house.

Meanwhile, Cindy's arms and legs were getting very, very, VERY tired.

She began to slip lower . . .

. . . and lower . . .

. . . and LOWER into the milk!

Just then, Frank knocked on Cindy's door.

He waited and waited. But no one came. 'Where can she be?' he thought.

While Frank was thinking, Cindy was sinking!

But she didn't stop splishing and splashing.

By now her arms and legs were getting very, very, very, VERY tired, indeed!

But something was changing.
The milk felt different.
It wasn't so runny!

Cindy was turning the milk into cream!

And the more she splished and splashed, the thicker it became . . .

Meanwhile, Frank was buzzing around the kitchen looking for Cindy.

He buzzed past Anita. 'Have you seen Cindy?' he asked.

'No,' said Anita. 'I'm looking for her, too! I want to tell her I'm sorry for calling her clumsy!'

Frank and Anita decided to search for Cindy together.

'Hold on tight!' said Frank.
And off they flew.

Back in the saucer, all Cindy's splashing had turned the milk into cream . . . and the cream into butter!

As soon as it was thick enough, Cindy climbed out.
'Thank goodness for all my arms and legs!' she puffed.

But when she tried to stand up . . .

. . . she slipped over again!

'Hee hee!' laughed Cindy, jumping back up.

Soon she was gliding . . .

. . . and spinning . . .

. . . and leaping!

And that was when Frank and Anita saw her.

'Hooray!' cried Anita. 'We've found her!'
'Wow!' gasped Frank. 'She's skating!'

Frank set Anita down on the edge of the saucer.

'I think you two need to talk,' he said. And he buzzed away.

‘I’m sorry I called you clumsy,’ said Anita. ‘I didn’t mean it!’
‘Well, you hurt my feelings,’ said Cindy.

‘I know,’ said Anita. ‘And you’re my friend!’

Cindy could see Anita meant it.

'That's OK,' she said.
'Are you sure?' asked Anita.
'I'm sure,' said Cindy. And she smiled.

Anita stepped on to the butter, to give Cindy a hug . . .

. . . BUT . . .

"BUMP!"

. . . she slipped over on to her bottom!

‘Come on, Anita!’ said Cindy. ‘I’ll teach YOU how to skate!’

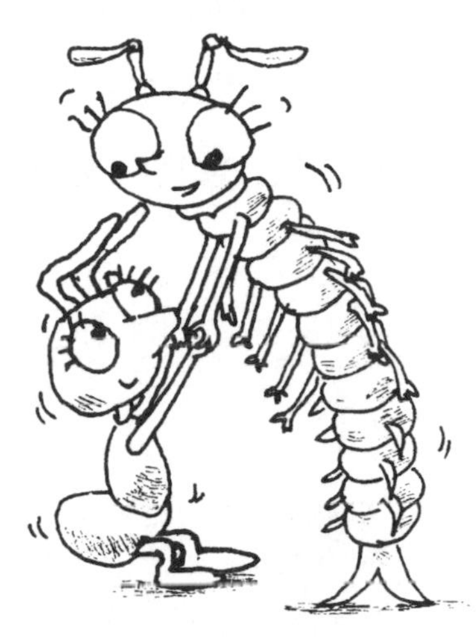

Meanwhile, Frank buzzed back to the sink.

He told everyone about Cindy, the skating centipede.

‘WOW!’ said the bugs.

They jumped out of the sink, and rushed over to the saucer.

When they saw Cindy, they clapped and cheered.

'How graceful she is!' they gasped. 'How does she do it?'

'Come and join in!' yelled Cindy.
'It's FUN!' shouted Anita.

One by one, the bugs stepped on to the butter . . .

They slipped . . .

. . . and tripped . . .

. . . and stumbled . . .

. . . and tumbled.

Soon the saucer was FULL of skating bugs . . .

But no one was as good as Cindy!

Then suddenly . . .

'Look out, everyone!' shouted Cindy.

Cindy and the other bugs jumped OUT of the saucer . . .

. . . and ran happily home.

Jimmy the cat stretched.

'Hmm,' he thought. 'That's the funniest looking milk I've ever seen!

But it still tasted good to him!

And as for Cindy . . .

She still knocked things over,
and tripped up now and then,
but no one called her clumsy,
not ever, ever again . . .